Handmade Secret Hiding Places

Handmade Secret Hiding Places
by Nonny Hogrogian

The Overlook Press · Woodstock, New York
The Bookstore Press · Lenox, Massachusetts

Published in 1975 by
The Overlook Press
Lewis Hollow Road
Woodstock, N.Y. 12498 and
The Bookstore Press
9 Housatonic Street
Lenox, Massachusetts 01240

ISBN: 0-87951-033-1
Library of Congress Catalog Card Number:
75-4379
Printed in the United States by
the studley press, inc.

For Mariah

Contents

The Mud House

Supplies: chicken wire (about
4 feet by 6 feet)
4 small wood
stakes
a hammer or mallet
a pail and shovel
earth mixed with weeds or sod
water

Hammer two stakes into the ground
through the short end of the chicken
wire. Bend the sheet of chicken wire into
the shape of an arc and hammer the other
two stakes through the other side of the
arc and into the ground.

Dig up some earth. Mix it with sod or
dry weeds. Wet it thoroughly. Scoop up

some wet earth by hand and begin to cover the chicken wire. Keep this up until all of the chicken wiring has been covered with the mud. Pat some dry weeds or grass onto the surface to hold the mud as it dries.

The mud house is ready.

The Pole Bean Teepee
(A Springtime project - a Summer hiding place)

Supplies: 5 or 6 strong branches about 1 inch
thick and 6 feet long
a piece of string or wire fastener
1 package of pole beans
a trowel or shovel
a rake

Pick a sunny place. This can be done in
your backyard or any small plot of land
about 4 feet around. Set the branches in
the ground in a circle. Bind them together
at the top with the string or wire.
Soften the soil around the bottom of
each branch with the trowel or shovel.
Then rake it smooth. Plant 3 or 4 beans

around each branch. Cover lightly with soil. Water them well.

Be sure to check them every day. Soon they will start to grow. Pull out any weeds that grow around them. Give them some water every day.

If you plant some flower seeds outside the teepee area you will have a little flower garden, too.

In two months your pole bean teepee will be ready to hide in and eat from. Invite friends for afternoon snacks. The beans will be delicious.

Behind the Stairs Hideout

Supplies: staircase which turns
with opening underneath
1 old sheet

This is a very simple hideout. All you have to do is tie one end of the long side of the sheet around a post at one end of the banister. Then tie the other end of the same side of the sheet to a post at the other end of the banister. See the picture on the facing page.

You can invite your friends and pets to your new hideout.

The Leafy Lean-to

Supplies: 2 trees a few feet apart
(with their lower branches
about 4 feet above the ground)
5 wooden posts or dowels or
strips of wood about 7 feet
long
many leafy branches

Place one wooden post across the lower
branches of the two trees. Lean the
other four posts against the first one as
shown in the drawing on the facing page.

Gather as many leafy twigs and branches as you can find. Weave them in and out of the posts until you have a thick roof of them.

Your lean-to is ready to play in.

The Cardboard Box House

Supplies: any large cardboard box such as
a mover's carton or a T.V. container
a pair of scissors
a pencil

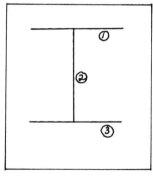

Draw three lines on one
side of a cardboard box as
shown in the diagram. Cut
through the cardboard
following the lines carefully.
Fold back the cardboard
from the center out.
Climb in. You can pull the shutters in
to keep your hideout a secret. You can
paint it inside and out, or cover it
with shelving paper.

The Four Poster Arabian Hideout

Supplies:
- 1 four poster bed
- 2 flat sheets
- 1 large fitted sheet
- 2 pillowcases
- 2 mops
- string

Do you have a bed with posts? And a large fitted sheet? If you do, you can make a perfect Arabian hideout.

Tie one end of a flat sheet to one headpost. Tie the other end of the long side of the sheet to the footpost. Do the same thing with another flat sheet to the other side of the bed. Fit the corners of the fitted sheet over the top of the four bed posts. Tie them on with a bit of string so they won't slip.

Take two mops. Cover the bottom of each with a pillow case and stand each on the bed to hold up the center of the fitted sheet.

Climb into your tent from the foot of the bed. You are the Sheik of your four poster Arabian hideout.

The Dugout

Supplies: a pail and shovel
a sandy beach

This one is easy. Just dig a nice big hole. If it begins to fill with water move back further from the shore's edge.

With a few friends to help you, you can make a dugout as wide as a room.

The String Hideout

Supplies: 1 or 2 big rolls of thick string
3 or 4 large trees or 1 very fat one
and 1 skinny one

Find a place that no one knows about except the animals. With the beginning of your string, tie a knot around the first tree trunk and walk around each of the other trees until you arrive back at the first tree.

Keep walking around the trees in the same direction placing one layer of string next to the last one. The closer together you place your string, the more secret your hideout will be.

When you have very little string left,

fasten the end to the closest tree trunk.
A few leafy branches will make a
beautiful roof.

Crawl in under the strings.
It's a secret.

Between the Chairs Hideout

Supplies: two armchairs
            a blanket or an old sheet

Here's a hideout you can make in the parlor or any room that contains two armchairs.

Push the two chairs around to face each other with standing room between them. Throw an old blanket or sheet over the chairs and that's all there is to it.

Climb in.

The After Christmas Tree Hideout

Supplies: a quiet corner of a building
four or five Christmas trees
thick gloves or mittens
a strong friend with mittens
or gloves
thick cord

This is a good hideout for scavengers.
The perfect time to make it is on the
day that the Christmas trees are
discarded. Pick four or five of the nicest
ones you can find, that are as close to
each other in size as possible.
        Carry one tree at a time (with your
friend) to a quiet corner. Be careful not
to drag them so as not to lose the needles.

Be sure to wear gloves or mittens to protect your hands from the sharp pine needles.

Gather the trees together. You can tie them at the top if they seem to need it. Lean them against the building for extra support.

The "After Christmas Tree Hideout" is ready for the new year.

How many other hiding places
can you make or find ?